Acting Edition

The Gumball Gang: Crime-Solving Kids

Book, Music & Lyrics
by Jim Colleran

concord
theatricals

No one shall make any changes in this title(s) for the purpose of production. No part of this book may be reproduced, stored in a retrieval system, scanned, uploaded, or transmitted in any form, by any means, now known or yet to be invented, including mechanical, electronic, digital, photocopying, recording, videotaping, or otherwise, without the prior written permission of the publisher. No one shall share this title(s), or any part of this title(s), through any social media or file hosting websites.

For all inquiries regarding motion picture, television, online/digital and other media rights, please contact Concord Theatricals Corp.

MUSIC AND THIRD-PARTY MATERIALS USE NOTE

Licensees are solely responsible for obtaining formal written permission from copyright owners to use copyrighted music and/or other copyrighted third-party materials (e.g. artworks, logos) in the performance of this play and are strongly cautioned to do so. If no such permission is obtained by the licensee, then the licensee must use only original music and materials that the licensee owns and controls. Licensees are solely responsible and liable for clearances of all third-party copyrighted materials, including without limitation music, and shall indemnify the copyright owners of the play(s) and their licensing agent, Concord Theatricals Corp., against any costs, expenses, losses and liabilities arising from the use of such copyrighted third-party materials by licensees. For music, please contact the appropriate music licensing authority in your territory for the rights to any incidental music.

IMPORTANT BILLING AND CREDIT REQUIREMENTS

If you have obtained performance rights to this title, please refer to your licensing agreement for important billing and credit requirements.

THE GUMBALL GANG: CRIME-SOLVING KIDS was first produced by TADA! Youth Theater in New York City on July 5, 2007. The performance was directed by Janine Nina Trevens and choreographed by Joanna Greer, with musical direction by Jim Colleran, sets by Ian Wallace, costumes by Mark Richard Caswell, and lighting design by Kirk Bookman. The Production Stage Manager was Beth Slepian. The cast was as follows:

CANDY KRUNCH . . . . Maya Park

DANNY . . . . Javier Cardenas

JESS . . . . Katherine Lerner Lee

ZAK . . . . Robert Aviles

PARKER . . . . Christina Franklin

BECCA KRUNCH . . . . Gabriela Gross

OLIVE KRUNCH . . . . Lindsey Estevez

LYDIA LEE . . . . Casey Wenger-Schulman

MORGAN MCCORGAN . . . . Nicholas Stewart

VICTORIA LASALLE . . . . Jasmine Perez

WINSTON WINSTON III . . . . Merce Jessor

TJ DOYLE . . . . Jennifer Wais

SQUEAK . . . . Taylor Jones

FRANCOIS . . . . Alec Cohen

ISABEL . . . . Ines Renique

GERTA . . . . Taylor Hogan

YVETTE . . . . Natalie Northup Bergner

RHONDA . . . . Nicole Carrington

KEISHA . . . . Saleema Josey

CHARITY ARMSTRONG . . . . Alex Getlin

ABBY ARMSTRONG . . . . Natalie Amaya

ETHAN ARMSTRONG . . . . Rovin Sena

QUENTIN . . . . Monk Boyewa Washington

HANNAH . . . . Sophie Silverstein

NORA . . . . Jarena Lee

THEO . . . . Anthony Sanchez

CHARACTERS

THE GUMBALL GANG

CANDY KRUNCH – Female; leader; organized, smart, fair-minded

DANNY/DANI – Athlete; agile, fit, a bit sarcastic and funny

JESS – Intellectual; into math, history, etc., "book-smart"

ZAK/ZOE – Altruist; great people skills, ray of sunshine, all heart; great singer

PARKER – Techie; into computers and gadgets; inventive and funny

KLUTZES

BECCA KRUNCH – Female; klutzy and self-deprecating but unflappable and likable

OLIVE/OLIVER KRUNCH – Devoted to Becca, supportive and relentlessly upbeat

REPORTERS

LYDIA LEE – Female; newshound; professional, perseverant and determined

MORGAN MCCORGAN – Reporter/photographer; ambitious and skeptical

VILLAINS

VICTORIA LASALLE – Female; beauty queen; vain and self-absorbed but intelligent

WINSTON WINSTON III – Male; rich kid; snobbish and elitist, hangs with Victoria

TJ DOYLE – Bully; dumb, cruel, resentful, hates the Gumball Gang

SQUEAK – TJ's sidekick; a tiny lackey, the smaller the better

ART STUDENTS

FRANCIS/FRANCES – Art student; fan of French Impressionism (Claude Monet, Edgar Degas, etc.)

ISABEL – Female; art student; fan of Mexican Folk Art (Frida Kahlo, Diego Rivera, etc.)

GUTHRIE – Art student; fan of Neo-modernism (Andy Warhol, Jackson Pollock, etc.)

JUDGES

(Resemble a 60s girl group)

YVETTE – Female; ringleader, tough, smart and fair; lower voice

RHONDA – Female; tough, smart and soulful; middle voice

KEISHA – Female; tough, smart and cool; upper voice

PROTESTERS

ABBY ARMSTRONG – Female; earnest and determined environmentalist

UNA/UPTON ARMSTRONG – Committed but somewhat cynical environmentalist

SKATER(S)

EMMETT/EMMA HANLEY – Skater dude; thrill-seeking, chill, honest

ADDITIONAL SKATERS – Optional roles; athletic kids with a variety of personalities

AUTHOR'S NOTES

The Gumball Gang is an "ensemble cast" show where every kid onstage is a suspect! No one should be anonymous; everyone should be part of a "suspect group."

To expand the cast beyond twenty-two performers, add additional **SKATERS**, **PROTESTERS** and/or **JUDGES**, and feel free to name the additional characters in your program. For those looking for a reduced cast, the **JUDGES** can be combined into one or two role(s) instead of three, and the **SKATERS** can be reduced to just **EMMETT**.

One actor doubles as the **CAT BURGLAR** in the Prologue.

SETTING

Town square and Krunch's candy store in Littletown, U.S.A.

TIME

The recent past.

MUSICAL NUMBERS

1.   Prologue . . . . Instrumental
2.   Gumball Gang . . . . Company
2a. Big Case Transition . . . . Instrumental
3.   Big Case . . . . Gumball Gang
3a. Big Scoop/Big Case . . . . Reporters & Gumball Gang
3b. Big Scoop (Reprise) . . . . Reporters
3c. Big Scoop Playoff . . . . Instrumental
4.   Cosmopolitan Fine Art Show . . . . Judges
4a. Gumball Transition 1 . . . . Instrumental
5.   The Blue-Tailed Skink . . . . Protesters & Company
6.   Trouble . . . . TJ, Squeak & Company
6a. Trouble Playoff . . . . Instrumental
7.   Follow Every Clue . . . . Gumball Gang & Company
7a. Follow Playoff . . . . Instrumental
7b. Follow Every Clue (Reprise) . . . . Gumball Gang
8.   Klutz . . . . Becca
9.   Work It Out . . . . Company
9a. Work It Out Playoff . . . . Instrumental
10. All for Me . . . . Victoria & Winston
10a. Gumball Transition 2 . . . . Instrumental
10b. Masterpiece Transition . . . . Instrumental
11. It's a Masterpiece . . . . Art Students
11a. Masterpiece Playoff . . . . Instrumental
12. Life Is Sweet . . . . Zak, Victoria, Winston & Gumball Gang
12a. Gumball Transition 3 . . . . Instrumental
12b. Cosmopolitan (Reprise) . . . . Judges
12c. Accusations . . . . Instrumental
13. Case Closed . . . . Company
14. Bows . . . . Company
15. Exit Music . . . . Instrumental

Appendix:
4.   Cosmopolitan Fine Art Show (Unis. Vers.) . . . . Judges

Prologue

[MUSIC NO. 01 – PROLOGUE: THE CAT BURGLAR]

(Summertime in a cheerful American suburb. Night. Low mysterious music. A **CAT BURGLAR**, *dressed in black, silently sneaks onstage. She moves effortlessly, a la "The Pink Panther," until she discovers what she's looking for – a porcelain doll. She takes a look-alike doll from her own velvet bag, switches it with the original, and begins to head out, when...)*

(Lights up on final note, revealing the **GUMBALL GANG** *surrounding the thief.)*

CANDY. Hold it right there.

CAT BURGLAR. Wait...this isn't what it looks like.

PARKER. Really? 'Cause it looks like you just stole that antique doll.

DANNY. And now it looks like you're busted.

CAT BURGLAR. By you? Who are you?

CANDY. People call us...

GUMBALL GANG. The Gumball Gang!

[MUSIC NO. 02 – GUMBALL GANG]

(Two **REPORTERS** *appear in front of a title card reading "Littletown Live!" They address the audience.)*

LYDIA. Breaking news! The Gumball Gang has done it again! Candy Krunch and her band of amateur sleuths have solved another crime. Morgan?

MORGAN. That's right, Lydia. Eleven crimes solved in the last year alone. And to think, it all began right here…

> *(As they sing, the* **GUMBALL GANG** *mimes the action described, eventually joining the song.)*

LYDIA.

JUST A COUPLE OF YEARS AGO,
THERE WAS A BULLY AND HER TWIN
AND THEY CONSPIRED TO BREAK IN
TO THE KRUNCH'S CANDY STORE.

MORGAN.

CANDY LET ALL HER BUDDIES KNOW,
AND THEY DECIDED TO PREPARE
BY SETTING UP A LITTLE SNARE,
ROLLING GUMBALLS ON THE FLOOR.

SKATER(S).

THEY SAVED THE DAY
AND EARNED QUITE A BIT OF FAME
AND ACCLAIM.

REPORTERS & SKATER(S).

AND THAT'S THE WAY
THESE YOUTHFUL DETECTIVES CAME
TO EARN THEIR NAME:

ENSEMBLE.

GUMBALL GANG!
THEY HAD SOLVED A CRIME WITH BRAINS AND
    INNOVATION!
GUMBALL GANG!
AS THE ROBBERS TRIPPED THEIR HEELS AND FLIPPED
    THEIR LIDS,

CLEVER CANDY KNEW
THAT HER FAITHFUL CREW
HAD SEALED THEIR REPUTATION
AS THE GUMBALL GANG!
CRIME SOLVING KIDS.

ABBY.
EV'RYBODY IN TOWN BEGAN
TO SEE THE GUMBALL GANG'S SUCCESS,
AND THEY WOULD SEND AN S.O.S.
ANY TIME THEY WERE IN NEED.

CAT BURGLAR.
CANDY AND HER AMAZING CLAN
WERE ALWAYS THERE TO HEED THEIR CALL
BY SOLVING ANY CRIME AT ALL,
SATISFACTION GUARANTEED!

TJ & SQUEAK.
THEY'LL SOLVE A CASE
OR TRACK DOWN A MISSING PET –

SQUEAK. *(Spoken in rhythm.)*
IT'S NO SWEAT!

PROTESTORS, CAT BURGLAR, TJ & SQUEAK.
SO, IF YOU FACE
A MYSTERY, YOU CAN BET
ON THIS QUINTET!

ENSEMBLE.
GUMBALL GANG!
THEY'RE THE KIDS TO CALL WHENEVER THERE IS
    TROUBLE.
GUMBALL GANG!
WHEN A CROOK COMMITS A CRIME THE LAW FORBIDS,
THEY WILL SEARCH AND SPY
AND PROBE AND PRY
AND CATCH THEM ON THE DOUBLE!
THEY'RE THE

GROUP 1.
> GUMBALL GANG...

GROUP 2.
> GUMBALL GANG...

GROUP 3.
> GUMBALL GANG!

ENSEMBLE.
> CRIME SOLVING KIDS.
>
> > *(Spoken in rhythm.)*
>
> THERE'S JESS!

JESS.
> I LIKE MATH AND SCIENCE, HISTORY AND LANGUAGE ARTS.

ENSEMBLE. *(Spoken in rhythm.)*
> PARKER!

PARKER.
> JUST FOR FUN, I TRY INVENTING THINGS WITH MOVING PARTS.

ENSEMBLE. *(Spoken in rhythm.)*
> DANNY!

DANNY.
> GIVE ME A CHANCE TO LEAP OR CLIMB OR SWIM OR JUMP OR RUN.

ENSEMBLE. *(Spoken in rhythm.)*
> ZAK!

ZAK.
> I SEEM TO CONNECT WITH PEOPLE, SPREADING JOY TO EV'RYONE!

ENSEMBLE.
> THERE'S JUST ONE MORE IN THE BUNCH:
> SHE'S THEIR LEADER, CANDY KRUNCH!
> CANDY KRUNCH!

CANDY.

> I'M ORGANIZED AND SYSTEMIZED
> 'CAUSE LOGIC IS THE KEY.
> NOW, COME ON, GANG,
> WE CAN'T JUST HANG,
> LET'S SOLVE A MYSTERY!

GUMBALL GANG.

> AND YOU KNOW WE'LL ALWAYS BE
> THE...

GUMBALL GANG.	**ENSEMBLE.**
GUMBALL GANG!	GUMBALL GANG!
WE'RE THE KIDS TO CALL WHENEVER THERE IS TROUBLE!	THEY'RE THE KIDS TO CALL WHENEVER THERE IS TROUBLE!
GUMBALL GANG!	GUMBALL GANG!
WHEN A CROOK COMMITS A CRIME THE LAW FORBIDS,	WHEN A CROOK COMMITS A CRIME THE LAW FORBIDS,
WE WILL SEARCH AND SPY	THEY WILL SEARCH AND SPY
AND PROBE AND PRY	AND PROBE AND PRY
AND CATCH THEM ON THE DOUBLE!	AND CATCH THEM ON THE DOUBLE!
WE'RE THE	THEY'RE THE

GROUP 1.

> GUMBALL GANG...

GROUP 2.

> GUMBALL GANG...

GROUP 3.

> GUMBALL GANG!

ALL.

> THE FAMOUS...
> CRIME SOLVING KIDS!

Scene One: The Candy Store

[MUSIC NO. 02A – BIG CASE TRANSITION]

(The Candy Store, Krunch's Confectioners. **JESS** *is deeply absorbed in a textbook,* **PARKER** *is working on some kind of electronic device, and* **DANNY** *is doing stretches.* **ZAK** *enters.)*

ZAK. Hey, Danny!

DANNY. Hey, Zak.

ZAK. What's up?

DANNY. Oh, the usual. Parker is busy inventing The Next Great Thing That'll Change Our Lives Forever...

PARKER. *(Engrossed in their work.)* And this one will, if I can just get the middleware to form real-time access to the data source.

DANNY. Whatever. And Jess is deeply absorbed in the Hundred Years War.

JESS. Almost done... I'm up to year ninety-nine.

ZAK. So where's Candy?

CANDY. *(Entering.)* Right here. I just went in back to get more rock candies. Gramps was right – rock candy is selling way better since we renamed the flavors Punk, Metal and Emo.

ZAK. Well, I'm glad the candy business is good, 'cause the crime-solving business is lame.

DANNY. I know. It's been, like, six months since we've solved a case.

JESS. Actually, it's been five months, twenty-one days, sixteen hours and *(Looks at watch.)* seven minutes.

DANNY. I was just gonna say that.

PARKER. You know, since the case of the decoy dolly, we haven't had a single lead.

CANDY. Don't worry. Something'll turn up. Till then, we're gonna repaint the store!

(They look skeptical.)

What? It'll be fun. First step: we've gotta clear out some of this stuff.

(General groans.)

ZAK. I'll help – I don't mind.

CANDY. Thanks, Zak. And Becca and Olive can help, too.

PARKER. Your cousins?

CANDY. Yeah. They're staying with me this week. I'm meeting them this afternoon.

DANNY. Isn't Becca the one who's kinda accident-prone?

JESS. Maybe we should keep her away from the glass case.

CANDY. She'll be fine. At least when Becca's around, things get exciting.

PARKER. And we could use some excitement around here.

[MUSIC NO. 03 – BIG CASE]

CANDY. Tell me about it.

GUMBALL CREW,
WE'VE GOT NOTHING TO DO,
AND WE'VE GOTTA GET BACK INTO
THE RACE.

ZAK.

GUMBALL GUYS,
WE'RE JUST SWATTING AT FLIES.

JESS.

WE'RE BECOMING A PRIVATE EYE'S
DISGRACE!

PARKER.

LET'S PUT ON A DISGUISE AND BE SPIES...

DANNY.

AND GET OUT OF THIS PLACE!

GUMBALL GANG.

THERE'S A PROBLEM THAT WE'VE ALL GOTTA FACE:
WE NEED A BIG CASE!

      (**REPORTERS** *enter.*)

LYDIA. Hey there, Gumball Gang!

MORGAN. Working on any good cases?

DANNY. Nope, nothing.

LYDIA. Come on. You have to give us something, or our show will be cancelled.

ZAK. Cancelled? But *Littletown Live!* is the best show on school TV!

MORGAN. Thanks, but the video club said we're out if we don't come up with some real news soon.

LYDIA. And if we can't succeed on middle-school-closed-circuit TV, how will we ever make it to cable?

CANDY. Well, we'd love to help, but we have nothing... except some new Indie Rock Candy.

LYDIA. No, thanks. We've gotta hit the street and find a story.

ZAK. Good luck!

[MUSIC NO. 3A – BIG SCOOP/BIG CASE]

Scene Two: Town Square

(**REPORTERS** *step outside of the Candy Store.*)

LYDIA. So, what now? Back to the police station for ideas?

MORGAN. We just came from there! We need to stop and think.

(**LYDIA** *sits while* **MORGAN** *paces.*)

NOTHING WE CAN USE EVER HAPPENS IN THIS TOWN.
WE TRY TO FIND THE NEWS, BUT THERE'S NOTHING
　　GOING DOWN!
JUST STROLLERS AND BOWLERS, AND GARDEN CLUB, TOO.
PLUS TYKES, BIKES – NOTHING NEW!
THIS LAZY AFTERNOON IS THE DULLEST OF THE YEAR.
PLEASE, SOMETHING HAPPEN SOON, OR OUR JOBS'LL
　　DISAPPEAR!
WE'LL SIT AND WAIT ON OUR FRONT STOOP WHILE WE
　　REGROUP.
YOU KNOW WHAT WE NEED?
A BIG...SCOOP!

LYDIA.

WE NEED A BIG SCOOP!
WE NEED A BIG STORY!
WE NEED A BIG SUPER-DUPER FIGHT FOR LOVE AND
　　GLORY!
IT'S GOTTA HAVE COMEDY AND TRAGEDY AND SYMPATHY,
　　TOO.
IT'S GOTTA BE BRAINY, BUT ZANY, AND EDGY AND NEW!
WE NEED A BIG BREAK!
WE NEED A BIG HEADLINE!
OH, WHAT WILL IT TAKE FOR US TO MAKE
OUR LOOMING DEADLINE?

LYDIA.
> IT'S WAY TOO LATE TO SIT AND WAIT ON OUR FRONT
> > STOOP!
> YOU KNOW WHAT WE NEED?
> WE NEED A BIG...SCOOP!
> WE NEED A BIG

LYDIA.	**MORGAN.**	**GUMBALL GANG.**
SCOOP!	NOTHING WE CAN USE	GUMBALL
WE NEED A BIG STORY!	EVER HAPPENS IN THIS TOWN.	CREW,
WE NEED A BIG SUPER- DUPER FIGHT FOR LOVE AND GLORY!	WE TRY TO FIND THE NEWS, BUT THERE'S NOTHING GOING DOWN.	WE'VE GOT NOTHING TO DO
IT'S GOTTA HAVE	JUST	AND WE'VE
COMEDY AND TRAGEDY	STROLLERS AND BOWLERS	GOTTA GET
AND SYMPATHY, TOO.	AND GARDEN CLUB, TOO.	BACK
IT'S GOTTA BE BRAINY, BUT ZANY, AND EDGY AND NEW!	PLUS TYKES, BIKES– NOTHING NEW!	INTO THE RACE!
WE NEED A BIG BREAK!	THIS LAZY AFTERNOON	GUMBALL
WE NEED A BIG HEADLINE!	IS THE THE DULLEST OF THE YEAR.	GUYS,
OH, WHAT WILL IT TAKE	PLEASE, SOMETHING	WE'RE JUST

FOR US TO MAKE
OUR LOOMING DEADLINE?
IT'S WAY TOO LATE TO SIT AND WAIT
ON OUR FRONT STOOP

HAPPEN SOON,
OR OUR JOBS'LL DISAPPEAR!
WE'LL SIT AND WAIT
ON OUR FRONT STOOP WHILE WE REGROUP.

SWATTING
AT FLIES.
THERE'S A PROBLEM
WE FACE.

REPORTERS.
YOU KNOW WHAT WE NEED?

GUMBALL GANG.
YOU KNOW WHAT WE NEED?

REPORTERS.
WE NEED A BIG...

GUMBALL GANG.
A BIG...

REPORTERS.
SCOOP!

GUMBALL GANG.
CASE!

REPORTERS.
BIG SCOOP!

GUMBALL GANG.
BIG CASE!

REPORTERS.
IF IT CAN'T BE, WE'RE GONNA SEE
OUR RATINGS DROOP...

GUMBALL GANG.
WE CAN'T WAIT

AROUND AND PACE.

LYDIA. *(Spoken in rhythm.)*
DO WE CONCEDE?

CANDY. *(Spoken in rhythm.)*
DO WE CONCEDE?

MORGAN. *(Spoken in rhythm.)*
WE DO, INDEED!

GUMBALL GANG (EXCEPT CANDY). *(Spoken in rhythm.)*
WE DO, INDEED!

ALL.
WE'LL BEG AND PLEAD IF ONLY WE'D
SOMEHOW SUCCEED AND FIND A LEAD.
SO, IT'S AGREED:
WE REALLY NEED
A BIG...

REPORTERS.
SCOOP!

GUMBALL GANG.
BIG CASE!

CANDY. I've gotta go meet Becca and Olive. You guys wanna come?

JESS. I'm in!

DANNY. Sure. Beats cleaning!

*(The **GANG** exits. **REPORTERS** remain.)*

LYDIA. Well, there goes the Gumball Gang.

MORGAN. And there goes our hope for a scoop.

*(Suddenly the doors to the museum fling open, and three colorfully-dressed **ART STUDENTS** emerge, speaking very excitedly.)*

FRANCIS. Wow...that painting was amazing! Almost as groundbreaking as Claude Monet.

ISABEL. Or Frida Kahlo.

GUTHRIE. Or Jackson Pollock.

FRANCIS. Everyone will be talking about it.

MORGAN. Talking about what? What's going on?

ISABEL. Oh, we just saw the most brilliant painting.

GUTHRIE. *(Noticing the notepads, etc.)* Are you reporters?

MORGAN. Yes… Morgan McCorgan and Lydia Lee from *Littletown Live!* And you are?

FRANCIS. I'm Francis.

ISABEL. I'm Isabel, and this is Guthrie.

GUTHRIE. We're visual art students at Mega City Art Academy.

FRANCIS. We came to Littletown to enter the big art competition.

LYDIA. Art competition?

ISABEL. Yes, the museum's sponsoring a competition for kids.

GUTHRIE. It's all part of their unveiling of Borislav DelaGriofski's masterpiece, *Expression.*

FRANCIS. As art students, we got a sneak preview of the painting. It's amazing!

ISABEL. The public unveiling is on Tuesday.

GUTHRIE. But since you're press, you can probably see it in advance.

LYDIA. *(Taking notes.)* Great! De-la-Gri-of-ski?

 (They nod.)

And what makes his work so great?

FRANCIS. First, his use of color. And shape. And of course, the signature.

ISABEL. DelaGriofski always signs his canvases on the back… no two alike.

GUTHRIE. We should get going, though. We need to prepare for the competition.

LYDIA. Okay... thanks for the lead.

MORGAN. But first, let me take a photo!

> *(The* **ART STUDENTS** *pose, and* **MORGAN** *snaps a picture. They momentarily blink or rub their eyes from the flash, then begin to exit.)*

Thanks!

ART STUDENTS. *(Ad-lib.)* See you tomorrow! / Bye! / Nice to meet you!, etc.

> *(The* **ART STUDENTS** *exit.)*

MORGAN. Wow, an art competition!

LYDIA. And a world-famous masterpiece! You know what this means...

[MUSIC NO. 03B – BIG SCOOP (REPRISE)]

LYDIA.
> WE FOUND A BIG LEAD!
> WE FOUND A SENSATION!

MORGAN.
> WE FOUND A GREAT DEED OF SUCH EXCEEDING
>   INSPIRATION!

REPORTERS.
> NOW, YOU CAN BET
> WE'LL NEVER LET OUR RATINGS DROOP!
> YOU KNOW WHAT WE GOT?
> A REALLY BIG SCOOP!

[MUSIC NO. 03C – BIG SCOOP PLAYOFF]

Scene Three: The Museum Steps

(A **CROWD** *is bustling about, socializing in front of the museum. The* **JUDGES** *stand on a platform, preparing for their speech. Some of the* **GUMBALL GANG** *is present, along with the other* **TOWN KIDS**. *The* **REPORTERS** *are taking notes and occasionally taking flash photos.)*

*(***CANDY**, **BECCA** *and* **OLIVE** *enter.)*

BECCA. Candy, I'm so sorry you had to wait at the station.

CANDY. No worries, Becca. Oh, look – there's Zak and Parker.

BECCA. *(To* **OLIVE**.*)* Don't let me hurt anybody.

OLIVE. I promise, big sister. I've got your back.

BECCA. Hey, you guys!

*(***BECCA** *moves towards the* **GANG**, *but bumps into someone, loses her balance, and falls to the floor.)*

I thought you said you had my back.

OLIVE. Sorry. But you did that from the front.

*(***VICTORIA** *and* **WINSTON** *approach the* **GUMBALL GANG**. *They are both quite well dressed.* **VICTORIA** *wears a pageant outfit, complete with tiara and sash.)*

VICTORIA. Why, Candy Krunch! What are you doing here? Shouldn't you be minding your litte store?

CANDY. Hi, Victoria. My grandfather's watching the store, thanks.

VICTORIA. Work, work, work! I don't know how the little people do it. Do you, Winston?

WINSTON. Victoria, some people were simply born to do manual labor, whereas we were born to supervise them.

PARKER. *(To* **VICTORIA.***)* What's with the tiara? Is that thing, like, permanently glued to your head?

VICTORIA. It is lovely, isn't it? I got it last week when I was named Little Miss Littletown. Well, gotta run. Come on, Winston… Let's get closer to the spotlight, where I belong.

> *(They move towards the stage as* **TJ** *and* **SQUEAK** *emerge from the crowd.)*

TJ. Well…if it isn't Candy Crumb and her buddies, the Dumbball Gang.

CANDY. Great. TJ Doyle…

SQUEAK. And Squeak!

CANDY. …and his sidekick, Squeak.

TJ. So, are you, like, suddenly big artists? Like Leopardo the Itchy or whatever?

SQUEAK. You mean Leonardo da Vinci?

TJ. I said "whatever."

ZAK. Actually, TJ, we're not artists. Just kids, trying to help people.

TJ. *Help* people? So you were *helping* my sisters when you sent them to reform school?

CANDY. TJ, it's not our fault the twins robbed the candy store.

DANNY. And it's not our fault you can't pronounce Leonardo da Vinci.

TJ. Just stay out of my face, Dumbball Gang. And be careful, 'cause I am wise as a rocket and quick as a judge.

[MUSIC NO. 04 – COSMOPOLITAN FINE ART SHOW]

(The **GUMBALL GANG** *reacts to TJ's error as* **TJ** *rejoins the crowd. A fanfare plays and the* **JUDGES** *appear.)*

YVETTE. Ladies and Gentlemen, may we have your attention...

GATHER AROUND,
YES, ONE AND ALL,
YOU ARE INVITED.
WE KNOW YOU ARE BOUND
TO BE ENTHRALLED
AND SO EXCITED.
WE'RE HERE TO ASTOUND YOU
WITH AN AMAZING PROPOSITION:

JUDGES.

IT'S THE COSMOPOLITAN FINE ART SHOW
AND AMATEUR COMPETITION!

RHONDA.

COME OUT AND SEE
THE WORK OF LATE
AND CURRENT MASTERS.

KEISHA & YVETTE.

COME AND SEE!

RHONDA.

YOU CAN FEEL FREE
TO THINK THEY'RE GREAT
OR JUST DISASTERS!

KEISHA & YVETTE.

IT'S GONNA BE

RHONDA.

IT'S ALL GONNA BE

JUDGES.

BIG NEWS!

RHONDA.

CHECK THE LATE EDITION

JUDGES.

FOR THE COSMOPOLITAN FINE ART SHOW
AND AMATEUR COMPETITION!

RHONDA & YVETTE.

OOH...

KEISHA.

YOU CAN PARTICIPATE, TOO,
BY MAKING YOUR OWN WORK OF ART.

RHONDA & YVETTE.

MAKE YOUR OWN ART...

KEISHA.

MAKE SOMETHING THAT REALLY SHOWS YOU,
WITH BEAUTY THAT COMES FROM THE HEART.

YVETTE.

MAKE A PAINTING,

RHONDA.

A SKETCH,

KEISHA.

OR A SCULPTURE!

JUDGES.

WE LEAVE THAT TO YOUR OWN DISCRETION.
BUT WHATEVER YOU CREATE
MUST INCORPORATE
OUR UNIVERSAL THEME
OF "EXPRESSION"!

YVETTE. The winning piece will tour the world...

RHONDA. Then return to the Cosmopolitan for all time.

KEISHA. Plus, the winner receives a year's supply of free candy from Krunch's Confectioners!

(*The* **CROWD** *cheers.*)

JUDGES.
IT'S GOTTA BE FUN,
SO GIVE IT HEART
AND HUMOR, TOO-OO.
AND WHEN YOU ARE DONE,
YOU WILL HAVE ART
EXPRESSING YOU-OO!
THEN FRIDAY AT ONE,
WE'RE GONNA AWARD THE BEST SUBMISSION
TO THE COSMOPOLITAN FINE ART SHOW...

KEISHA. Deadline is Thursday at five p.m.!

JUDGES.
WHERE ALL THE PROMINENT ARTISTS GO...

YVETTE. Remember, everybody...be inventive!

JUDGES.
THE COSMOPOLITAN FINE ART SHOW
AND AMATEUR COMPETITION!

RHONDA & YVETTE.
BEGIN!
LIFT YOUR CHIN,
START RIGHT IN!

KEISHA.
AND MAY THE BEST ART WIN!

JUDGES.
MAY THE BEST ART WIN!

(**MORGAN** *takes a flash picture, momentarily blinding the* **JUDGES**.)

YVETTE. Thanks again to Mr. Krunch for donating the candy. Unfortunately, employees of Krunch's Confectioners are ineligible.

DANNY. Oh, Candy…you can't enter.

CANDY. *(Cheerfully.)* It's all right – I knew.

YVETTE. *(Indicating an easel covered with a sheet.)* Remember, we'll unveil DelaGriofski's masterpiece tomorrow…

KEISHA. So, please return tomorrow, Tuesday, at ten a.m.

RHONDA. In the meantime, artists, get to work!

[MUSIC NO. 04A – GUMBALL TRANSITION 1]

Scene Four: Various Locations (Getting to Work)

(As the **CROWD** *disperses,* **REPORTERS** *address the audience.)*

LYDIA. Welcome to the new edition of *Littletown Live!* Well, Morgan, it's Monday afternoon and the art competition is underway!

MORGAN. That's right, Lydia. And young artists are already competing for that free candy!

LYDIA. Here's one now. Emmett, what are you making?

EMMETT. Dude, I love the excitement of a new challenge, so I'm making a sculpture from all my extreme sports equipment.

LYDIA. Great idea! Any other projects, Morgan?

(Characters appear as **REPORTERS** *mention them.)*

MORGAN. Well, we have Becca and Olive Krunch, who can't seem to decide.

OLIVE. *(Counting 1-2-3 on fingers.)* How 'bout...stained glass, a mobile, macaroni art?

BECCA. *(Also counting 1-2-3 on fingers.)* Nah... I'd break it; I'd tangle it; I'd eat it.

MORGAN. Then there's Winston Winston the Third and Victoria LaSalle.

VICTORIA. Just sketch me, Winston... You'd be doing a public service.

WINSTON. My sketches are for me, Victoria, not the general public. Besides, I'd rather listen to my antique records.

VICTORIA. Records! You are *so* last century.

LYDIA. Of course, we also have our visiting art students...

GUTHRIE. The greatest artists were visionaries. Andy Warhol made art that broke barriers.

FRANCIS. Sure, but the French masters, like Monet or Degas, captured beauty and light.

ISABEL. Yes, but Mexican folk artists, like Frieda Kahlo and Diego Rivera, made art that depicted humanity.

GUTHRIE. But art's about innovation!

FRANCIS. It's about beauty!

ISABEL. It's about people!

LYDIA. It's about *time* you three stop arguing and start creating.

MORGAN. We'll continue our coverage / later today...

(**MORGAN** *is interrupted by* **PROTESTERS**, *who enter with a sign saying, "SAVE THE SKINK." They chant as they march in.*)

PROTESTERS. Save the blue-tailed skink! Save the blue-tailed skink!

LYDIA. Uh...Morgan, what's going on over there?

MORGAN. Looks like a civil demonstration.

(*To* **PROTESTERS**.) What's all this about?

ABBY. Hi, I'm Abby Armstrong...

UNA. And I'm her sister, Una.

ABBY. And we're here to spread awareness of the blue-tailed skink.

PROTESTERS. (*Shouting.*) Save the blue-tailed skink!

MORGAN. The what?

UNA. The skink. It's a type of salamander.

ABBY. You see, DelaGriofski made his blue paint from endangered plants and animals, so we're here to protest.

MORGAN. So, you're not entering the contest?

UNA. No, we're still entering. We're making a completely organic eco-chart of endangered wildlife.

ABBY. And you know what's at the top?

MORGAN. The blue-tailed skink?

ABBY. Exactly. We even wrote a song to help you remember.

[MUSIC NO. 05 – THE BLUE-TAILED SKINK]

ABBY & UNA.
THE BLUE-TAILED SKINK,
THE BLUE-TAILED SKINK.
THOSE POOR ANIMALS ARE ON THE BRINK.
BEFORE YOU PAINT WITH YOUR BLUE INK,
STOP AND THINK ABOUT THE BLUE-TAILED SKINK!

UNA. The Australian blue-tailed skink no longer exists in the wild.

ABBY. They only live in wildlife refuges!

MORGAN. Why?

UNA. We'll tell you!
SOME SEVEN MILLION YEARS AGO,
IN A LAND CALLED CHRISTMAS ISLAND,

ABBY.
SOME SHORT-LIMBED LIZARDS MADE THEIR WAY
FROM THE LOWLAND TO THE HIGHLAND.

UNA.
UNLIKE OTHER LIZARDS
WHO HAD TAILS OF GRAYISH HUE,

ABBY.
> THESE SKINKS HAD TAILS
> WRAPPED IN SCALES
> OF VIBRANT ROYAL BLUE!

ABBY, UNA & SMALL GROUP.[*]
> THE BLUE-TAILED SKINK,
> THE BLUE-TAILED SKINK.
> THOSE POOR ANIMALS ARE ON THE BRINK.
> BEFORE YOU PAINT WITH YOUR BLUE INK,
> STOP AND THINK ABOUT THE BLUE-TAILED SKINK!

LYDIA. But what does that have to do with DelaGriofski's masterpiece?

UNA. Hang on, we'll tell you. *(To* **ABBY.***)* Some people are so impatient.

ABBY. I know.

UNA.
> ALTHOUGH FOR MANY CENTURIES
> THEIR DAYS WERE BRIGHT AND SUNNY,

ABBY.
> THOSE SKINKS GOT BURNED WHEN HUMANS LEARNED
> THEIR TAILS COULD EARN SOME MONEY.

UNA.
> THEIR LIVES WERE LOST TO PREDATORS
> WHO ROAMED WITHOUT RESTRAINT

ABBY.
> AND TO PAINTERS WHO
> USED THAT BLUE
> TO MAKE THEIR ROYAL PAINT!

ALL.
> THE BLUE-TAILED SKINK,
> THE BLUE-TAILED SKINK.

---

[*] As they become convinced, additional **ENSEMBLE** members join **ABBY** and **UNA** as **PROTESTERS.**

THOSE POOR ANIMALS ARE ON THE BRINK.
BEFORE YOU PAINT WITH YOUR BLUE INK,
STOP AND THINK ABOUT THE BLUE-TAILED SKINK!

ABBY & UNA.
AS FOR WHO'S RESPONSIBLE,
WE HATE TO SAY HIS NAME.

UNA. *(Spoken in rhythm.)*
IT'S DELAGRIOFSKI.

OTHER PROTESTERS. *(Spoken in rhythm.)*
DELAGRIOFSKI?

ALL.
HE'S THE ONE TO BLAME!

ABBY. *(Spoken in rhythm.)*
BUT IT'S NOT TOO LATE
TO SET THINGS RIGHT
IF WE ALL TRY WITH ALL OUR MIGHT.

UNA. *(Spoken in rhythm.)*
JUST HEED OUR PLEA
AND YOU WILL SEE,

ABBY & UNA.
THE FUTURE WILL BE BRIGHT!

ZAK. *(Spoken in rhythm.)*
HEY, EV'RYBODY!
LET'S ALL DANCE!

UNA. *(Spoken in rhythm.)*
YOU WANNA DANCE?!

ABBY & ZAK. *(Spoken in rhythm.)*
ALL RIGHT!

ALL. *(Spoken in rhythm.)*
WOO!

(Dance break: Eight counts of eight.)

ALL.
SAVE THE SKINK! SAVE THE SKINK!
SAVE THE BLUE-TAILED SKINK!

SAVE THE SKINK! SAVE THE SKINK!
SAVE THE BLUE-TAILED SKINK!

SAVE THE SKINK! SAVE THE SKINK!
SAVE THE BLUE-TAILED SKINK!

ABBY & UNA. *(Spoken in rhythm.)*
THANKS FOR JOINING IN OUR RHYME.
EV'RYBODY, ONE MORE TIME!

ALL.
THE BLUE-TAILED SKINK,
THE BLUE-TAILED SKINK.
THOSE POOR ANIMALS ARE ON THE BRINK.

GROUP 1.
THEY'RE NOT RED OR GREEN OR PINK!

GROUP 2.
THEY'RE WORSE OFF THAN YOU MAY THINK!

GROUP 3.
THEY'LL BE GONE IN HALF A WINK!

ABBY & UNA. *(Spoken in rhythm.)*
THINK OF THE BLUE-TAILED SKINK!

GROUP 1.
LET'S FORM A QUORUM...

GROUP 2.
AND CAMPAIGN FOR 'EM...

GROUP 3.
'CAUSE IF WE IGNORE 'EM

ALL.
THEY WILL BE EXTINC...T!

(Shouted.)

SAVE THE SKINK!

MORGAN. Hey, Armstrongs, let me get a picture.

> (**PROTESTERS** *pose with their signs and* **MORGAN** *takes a photograph. They rub their eyes, slightly disoriented by the flash.)*

PROTESTERS. Save the skink! Save the skink!

(They exit, chanting.)

MORGAN. So, lots of projects and a protest in the works! All for that candy...

LYDIA. No need to "sugarcoat" this one, Morgan, 'cause first prize is "sweet"! Remember, artists, it's a "rocky road" to the top, so use your "jellybeans," and "by gum," you'll be in for a "treat." Right, Morgan?

MORGAN. Uh, right.

LYDIA. Tomorrow, we'll return with the unveiling. Till then, this is Lydia Lee...

MORGAN. And Morgan McCorgan...

REPORTERS. For *Littletown Live!*

MORGAN. *(To* **LYDIA.***)* Did we really need all those candy puns?

LYDIA. Hey, if we want to go national, we've gotta kick it up. Let's go.

> (**REPORTERS** *exit as* **GUMBALL GANG** *enters, carrying paint supplies.)*

CANDY. You guys can still enter if you want.

ZAK. But it wouldn't be fun without you.

JESS. We only had a 6.2 percent chance of winning, anyway.

*(**TJ** and **SQUEAK** enter.)*

DANNY. Ugh. Hey, TJ.

TJ. Hey, Danny the Granny.

DANNY. *(Ready to start a fight.)* You know, TJ…

ZAK. *(Interrupting.)* Are you entering the contest?

TJ. No way. Contests are lame.

SQUEAK. Yeah. We're going to the park to play Frisbee, like we do every day.

TJ. And if anyone's in the way, I'll just take 'em out.

JESS. With your scintillating wit and customary panache?

TJ. Maybe, if I knew what that was.

[MUSIC NO. 06 – TROUBLE]

CANDY. So, you're really not gonna make anything?

TJ. We're gonna make what we always make.

GUMBALL GANG. What's that?

TJ & SQUEAK. Trouble.

COMPANY (EXCEPT TJ & SQUEAK).
THOSE KIDS ARE TROUBLE.
OH! DON'T DARE TO DISAGREE.
THOSE KIDS ARE TROUBLE.
CAN'T YOU SEE?
THEIR HATE AND ANGER ONLY WORSEN.
THEY'RE MEANER THAN A PERSON SHOULD BE…
THOSE KIDS ARE TROUBLE WITH A CAPITAL T.

TJ. That's right. T-R-U-B-B…wait…

COMPANY (EXCEPT TJ & SQUEAK). T-R-O-U-B-L-E.

TJ. That's what I said. T-R-O-B…

**COMPANY (EXCEPT TJ &
SQUEAK).**

T-R-O-U-B-L-E.

TJ.

Whatever!

TJ. *(Spoken in rhythm.*)*

WE'RE ROUGH!

SQUEAK.

WE'RE TOUGH!

TJ.

WE DON'T CARE ABOUT STUFF LIKE GRADES OR SCHOOL.

SQUEAK.

OR THE GOLDEN
RULE!

BROKEN!
LISTEN UP, TJ...

HAVE SPOKEN!
WE'RE NOT JOKIN'.

TJ.

RULES ARE FOR FOOLS,
  AND THEY'RE MADE TO
  BE BROKEN!

AND SQUEAK!
SPOKEN!

OUR DEEDS ARE FAMOUS.

TJ & SQUEAK.

EVEN THOUGH SOME PEOPLE IN THIS TOWN MIGHT
  BLAME US!

TJ.

YOU WON'T STOP ME.

SQUEAK.

OR ME!

TJ.

CAN'T YOU SEE?

TJ & SQUEAK.

WE'RE TROUBLE WITH A CAPITAL T!

---

* **TJ** and **SQUEAK** rap throughout "Trouble." Licensees should assume
all **TJ** and **SQUEAK** lyrics are spoken in rhythm.

COMPANY.

THOSE KIDS ARE TROUBLE.	**TJ & SQUEAK.** WE'RE TROUBLE.

COMPANY.

THOSE KIDS ARE
    TROUBLE.
OH! DON'T DARE TO
    DISAGREE.
THOSE KIDS ARE
    TROUBLE.
CAN'T YOU SEE?
THEIR HATE AND ANGER
    ONLY WORSEN
THEY'RE MEANER THAN A
    PERSON SHOULD BE...
THOSE KIDS ARE TROUBLE
    WITH A CAPITAL T.

TJ & SQUEAK.

WE'RE TROUBLE.

OH! DON'T DARE TO
    DISAGREE.
WE'RE
    TROUBLE.
CAN'T YOU SEE?
OUR HATE AND ANGER
    ONLY WORSEN.
WE'RE MEANER THAN A
    PERSON SHOULD BE...
WE'RE TROUBLE
    WITH A CAPITAL T.

TJ. For TJ.

SQUEAK. And Squeak.

COMPANY (EXCEPT TJ & SQUEAK).

T-R-O-U-B-L-E.

TJ.

WHEN THE GANG APPEARED,
MY NAME WAS SMEARED.

SQUEAK.

IT WAS WEIRD!

TJ.

THEY WERE CHEERED,
AND WE WERE NEVER CLEARED.

SQUEAK.

WHEN ALL THIS ENDS,
WE'RE GONNA BE REVERED.

TJ.

I DON'T WANNA BE FRIENDS...
I'D RATHER BE FEARED!

SQUEAK.

WE'RE GREAT!

TJ.

HERE'S HOW WE OPERATE:

SQUEAK.

WE HATE AND BERATE.

TJ.

AND STRAIGHT-UP DOMINATE!

SQUEAK. *(To* **TJ.***)*

THEY'LL SEE...

TJ. *(To* **SQUEAK.***)*

THAT YOU AND ME...

TJ & SQUEAK.

WE'RE TROUBLE WITH A CAPITAL T!

COMPANY (EXCEPT TJ &
SQUEAK).

THOSE KIDS ARE
TROUBLE.
OH! DON'T DARE TO
DISAGREE.
THOSE KIDS ARE
TROUBLE.
CAN'T YOU SEE?
THEIR HATE AND ANGER
ONLY WORSEN.
THEY'RE MEANER THAN A
PERSON SHOULD BE...
THOSE KIDS ARE TROUBLE
WITH A CAPITAL T.

TJ & SQUEAK.

WE'RE TROUBLE.

OH! DON'T DARE TO
DISAGREE.
WE'RE TROUBLE.

CAN'T YOU SEE?
OUR HATE AND ANGER
ONLY WORSEN
WE'RE MEANER THAN A
PERSON SHOULD BE...
WE'RE TROUBLE
WITH A CAPITAL T.

TJ.

DON'T MESS WITH ME!

SQUEAK.

DON'T MESS WITH *ME*!

ALL.
T-R-O-U-B-L-E.

SQUEAK. Hey, you said it right that time.

TJ. I know.

TJ & SQUEAK.
T-R-O-U-B-L-E!

TJ. Come on, Squeak...we've got people to go and places to meet.

SQUEAK. Later, losers!

[MUSIC NO. 06A – TROUBLE PLAYOFF]

Scene Five: The Museum Steps (The Unveiling)

(The **REPORTERS** *enter and address the audience. Behind them, everyone else gathers to watch the* **JUDGES** *prepare the unveiling.)*

LYDIA. Good morning, and welcome to the Tuesday edition of *Littletown Live!*

MORGAN. It's time to unveil DelaGriofski's masterpiece, *Expression.*

LYDIA. We saw the painting at a press briefing last night, and folks, you're in for a treat!

MORGAN. Let's watch...

YVETTE. Good morning, artists! We hope you're working hard on your projects for the contest.

KEISHA. Remember, all entries are due by five p.m. Thursday!

RHONDA. To inspire you, we're proud to present this early work of modern art.

YVETTE. Ladies and Gentlemen, the one and only... *Expression* by Borislav DelaGriofski!

(The **JUDGES** *remove a cloth cover from the easel. The painting is revealed to be a giant blue dot on a white background.)*

ISABEL. Fascinating!

GUTHRIE. Innovative!

ABBY. Destructive!

TJ. I don't get it.

DANNY. You know, TJ, for once I agree with you. I don't get it either.

WINSTON. Of course you don't. It's called geometric abstraction, and it's not meant for the common folk to understand.

TJ. Well, that's dumb, 'cause I could have painted that stupid blue circle myself.

WINSTON. See? Fine art is wasted on the masses.

JESS. It's not that complicated: DelaGriofski focused on emotional impact, not elaborate details.

ZAK. So, the point is – how does this make you feel?

JESS. Exactly.

VICTORIA. This is crazy. I'm far more attractive than that painting, and *it's* getting all the attention!

YVETTE. Ladies and Gentlemen, please note DelaGriofski's trademark signature, found here on the back of the canvas.

(**JUDGES** *turn the canvas to reveal the back.*)

KEISHA. Every DelaGriofski is signed in a different color, and this one is...dark purple?!?

(*The* **JUDGES** *gasp.*)

RHONDA. What? Everyone knows he used dark purple for *Meditation, Part Three.*

YVETTE. This painting is a fake! That can only mean one thing:

JUDGES. The Masterpiece has been stolen!

[MUSIC NO. 07 – FOLLOW EVERY CLUE]

(*Huge response from the* **CROWD.**)

LYDIA. (*To* **MORGAN.**) We've gotta get this to the network!

CANDY. Gumball Gang, you know what to do...

GUMBALL GANG.

FOLLOW, FOLLOW EACH CLU-UE...
FOLLOW, FOLLOW EACH CLU-UE.

CANDY.

WHY WOULD ANYONE COMMIT THIS CRIME?
WELL, WE DON'T HAVE TIME TO PONDER.
GOTTA GET THE FACTS AND KEEP IT BRIEF.
CAN'T ALLOW THAT THIEF TO WANDER.

GUMBALL GANG.

THE CASE WE'VE WAITED FOR
HAS LANDED HERE AT OUR FRONT DOOR!
QUICK – TAKE A LOOK AROUND
AND SEE WHAT CAN BE FOUND!
CHECK OUT EV'RY HAIR THAT'S OUT OF PLACE.
WE'RE GONNA CRACK THIS CASE!

GUMBALL GANG, WE GOT A JOB TO DO:
FOLLOW EV'RY CLUE
TILL THE CASE IS ENDED.
SEARCH HIGH AND LOW
'CAUSE THERE'S NO LEAD WE WON'T PURSUE.

TELL THE THIEF THEY MIGHT AS WELL ADMIT
WE WILL NEVER QUIT
TILL THEY'RE APPREHENDED.
WE ALL KNOW WHAT WE SHOULD DO...
FOLLOW EV'RY CLUE!

ENSEMBLE.

FOLLOW, FOLLOW EACH CLU-UE...

CANDY. Who are the prime suspects?

ENSEMBLE.

FOLLOW, FOLLOW EACH CLU-UE!

CANDY. Let's take them one by one.

DANNY.
> YOU CAN BET THE THIEF IS VERY BRIGHT—
> AND THAT WINSTON'S QUITE A SMARTIE.

CANDY. Good point.

PARKER.
> OR IT COULD BE ROTTEN TJ DOYLE,
> WHO JUST LOVES TO SPOIL A PARTY.

SQUEAK. And Squeak!

JESS.
> THEN THERE'S MISS BEAUTY QUEEN,
> WHO'S JEALOUS OF THIS WHOLE ART SCENE.

ZAK. *(Spoken in rhythm.)*
> OR GUTHRIE, FRANCIS,

> *(Sung.)*

> ISABEL –
> WHO KNOW THE ART SO WELL.

GUMBALL GANG.
> PLUS THE JUDGES, ARMSTRONGS, SKATERS,* TOO...
> OR EVEN ME AND YOU!

GUMBALL GANG.	**ENSEMBLE.**
GUMBALL GANG, WE GOT A JOB TO DO:	GUMBALL GANG, YOU GOT A JOB TO DO:
FOLLOW EV'RY CLUE	FOLLOW EV'RY CLUE
TILL THE CASE IS ENDED.	TILL THE CASE IS ENDED.
SEARCH HIGH AND LOW,	SEARCH HIGH AND LOW,
'CAUSE THERE'S NO LEAD WE WON'T PURSUE.	'CAUSE THERE'S NO LEAD YOU WON'T PURSUE.
TELL THE THIEF THEY MIGHT AS WELL ADMIT	TELL THE THIEF THEY MIGHT AS WELL ADMIT
WE WILL NEVER QUIT	YOU WILL NEVER QUIT
TILL THEY'RE APPREHENDED.	TILL THEY'RE APPREHENDED.

---

* If only one **SKATER**, substitute "EMMETT" for "SKATERS."

<table>
<tr><td>

WE ALL KNOW WHAT WE
    SHOULD DO...

</td><td>

WE ALL KNOW WHAT YOU
    SHOULD DO...

</td></tr>
</table>

GUMBALL GANG.

FOLLOW EV'RY CLUE!

ENSEMBLE.

FOLLOW, FOLLOW EACH CLU-UE...

GUMBALL GANG.

WE CAN'T RELY ON OUR OWN BIASED POINT OF VIEW.
WE'VE GOT TO TRY TO BE OBJECTIVE, FAIR AND TRUE.
WE'LL LEARN THE "WHY," THE "HOW,"
THE "WHAT," THE "WHEN," THE "WHO"!

GUMBALL GANG & ENSEMBLE.

SO PROBE AND PRY
AND SEARCH AND SPY
AND FOLLOW EV'RY CLUE!
EV'RY CLUE...

GUMBALL GANG.	**ENSEMBLE.**

GUMBALL GANG, WE GOT
    A JOB TO DO:
FOLLOW EV'RY CLUE
TILL THE CASE IS ENDED.
SEARCH HIGH AND LOW,
'CAUSE THERE'S NO LEAD
    WE WON'T PURSUE.
TELL THE THIEF THEY
    MIGHT AS WELL ADMIT
WE WILL NEVER QUIT
TILL THEY'RE
    APPREHENDED.
WE ALL KNOW WHAT WE
    SHOULD DO...
FOLLOW EV'RY CLUE!
	GUMBALL GANG, YOU GOT
	    A JOB TO DO:
	FOLLOW EV'RY CLUE
	TILL THE CASE IS ENDED.
	SEARCH HIGH AND LOW,
	'CAUSE THERE'S NO LEAD
	    YOU WON'T PURSUE.
	TELL THE THIEF THEY
	    MIGHT AS WELL ADMIT
	YOU WILL NEVER QUIT
	TILL THEY'RE
	    APPREHENDED.
	WE ALL KNOW WHAT YOU
	    SHOULD DO...
	FOLLOW EV'RY CLUE!

[MUSIC NO. 07A – FOLLOW PLAYOFF]

Scene Six: The Candy Store (Brainstorm/ Interviews)

(Lights up on the Candy Store. The **GUMBALL GANG** *is brainstorming.)*

CANDY. So, what have we got?

DANNY. One phony painting, one missing masterpiece, one very freaked-out museum, and a whole lot of suspects.

CANDY. Let's start with the fake painting. What would you need to make that?

JESS. I made a list. *(Reads.)* A canvas; blue, white and purple paint; a wide brush to paint the front; and a thin brush for the signature.

CANDY. Nice work. Anything else?

ZAK. That painting was perfectly round. You think most kids could do that?

DANNY. They could if they had something round to trace, like a plate, or – I don't know – a lampshade.

PARKER. Great. So we're looking for a paint-covered kid with a lampshade on their head.

CANDY. Of course, the thief also needed a motive.

ZAK. Well, anyone would want that painting for the money.

PARKER. Not Winston.

CANDY. But there are lots of expensive paintings in the museum. Why this one?

DANNY. What about the means? We've asked "Who?" and "What?" but not "How?"

PARKER. Or even "When?"

CANDY. Good point. The painting was stolen sometime between last night and this morning, because the judges showed it to the press last night.

PARKER. Are you sure they showed the real painting and not the fake one? This morning, they could barely tell the difference.

JESS. They'd know if they checked the signature.

CANDY. Only one way to know for sure...Let's get out there and gather some information. Gumball Gang, we are –

[MUSIC NO. 07B – FOLLOW EVERY CLUE (REPRISE)]

on the case!

GUMBALL GANG.
WE ALL KNOW WHAT WE SHOULD DO...
FOLLOW EV'RY CLUE!

Scene Seven: Becca and Olive

(**BECCA** *and* **OLIVE** *enter with art supplies.* **OLIVE***'s arm is bandaged.*)

BECCA. I'm so sorry, Olive. I really didn't think that stack of paint cans was so precarious.

OLIVE. It's okay. At least I don't need stitches.

BECCA. I don't know what happened. One second, I was reaching for purple paint, and suddenly, you were under a pile of cans.

OLIVE. Forget it, Becca. I'm fine. Plus, the hardware store guy gave us all this free stuff.

BECCA. Yeah. Now we just have to figure out what to make with it.

OLIVE. Maybe you can figure it out. I need a break.

BECCA. Okay, thanks. See you later.

(**OLIVE** *exits.*)

Come on, Becca. Do something right for a change. Just make something that expresses who you are.

[MUSIC NO. 08 – KLUTZ]

So, who am I? *(Sighs.)* That's easy...*

I KNOW PEOPLE SAY I'M CLUMSY,
KIND OF AN OAF, ALL-THUMBS-Y...
I WISH THAT I COULD SAY THEY'RE NUTS.

---

* Note: "Klutz" is an opportunity for the actress playing **BECCA** to show off her slapstick comedy chops. She should repeatedly trip, bump, and knock things over. Any attempt to remedy a mistake should only worsen the situation. Feel free to use lots of props.

BUT EV'RY PATH I SEE
ALWAYS SEEMS TO BE
FULL OF BUMPS AND RUTS.
I MIGHT AS WELL ADMIT,
HERE'S THE TRUTH OF IT: *(Music: Bonk! Bonk! Bonk!)*

(Spoken in rhythm.)
I'M A KLUTZ!

(Sung.)
WHEN I GO TO MAIL A LETTER,
I'LL GET MY BRAND-NEW SWEATER
CAUGHT IN THE DOOR JUST AS IT SHUTS.
AND WHEN I'M ON THE GO,
YOU CAN BET WITH NO
IFS OR ANDS OR BUTS,
I'LL SLIP, AND WITH A THUD,
LAND RIGHT IN THE MUD. *(Bonk! Bonk!)*
I'M A... *(Bonk! Bonk! Bonk!)*
KLUTZ!
I DREAM THAT I'M AS GRACEFUL AS A WILLOW,
LOVELY AS A SWAN UPON A POOL,
GLIDING LIKE A SILVER DOVE ABOVE THE SEA.
I SEEM TO BE AS GENTLE AS A PILLOW,
PERFECT AS A BRIGHT AND SHINY JEWEL.
IN THIS WORLD THAT I'VE CREATED,
I DON'T HAVE TO BE
UNCOORDINATED ME.
I WISH I COULD PROVE, JUST ONCE,
THAT I'M NOT A FUMBLING DUNCE –
THAT I'VE GOT A LOT OF BRAINS AND GUTS.
AND THAT'LL BE THE DAY
WHEN THE PEOPLE SAY,
"LOOK HOW BECCA STRUTS!

BECCA.

> SHE'S CONFIDENT AND PROUD
> MOVING THROUGH THE CROWD! *(Bonk!)*
>
> SHE'S ELEGANT AND BOLD,
> NIMBLE AND CONTROLLED!" *(Bonk! Bonk!)*
>
> UNTIL THAT COMES TO BE,
> SURELY, THEY'LL AGREE *(Bonk! Bonk! Bonk!)*
> THAT I'M...A *(Bonk! Bonk! Bonk! Bonk! Bonk! Bonk!)*
> KLUTZ!

Scene Eight: Investigating The Crime

MORGAN. Well, Lydia, it's Wednesday morning, and the thief remains at large.

LYDIA. Don't worry, Littletown. The Gumball Gang is interviewing suspects, and I'm sure they'll get to the bottom of this mystery.

[MUSIC NO. 09 – WORK IT OUT]

(Several tableaux, each with one **GUMBALL GANG** *member interviewing a different group. The groups unfreeze one by one to reveal parts of the interviews. First,* **CANDY** *and the* **JUDGES** *unfreeze.)*

CANDY. You're sure the painting you saw last night was authentic?

YVETTE. I'm certain. I checked it myself, before covering it up for the cameras.

CANDY. You didn't show the signature to the press?

KEISHA. Nope. We only showed the painting from the front.

RHONDA. We wanted to keep the name a surprise.

CANDY. It was a surprise all right.

ENSEMBLE.
YOU'RE ON A MISSION, BABY:
GATHER UP THE FACTS AND FIND A…LEAD!
USE INTUITION, BABY.
THERE'S A LOT OF KIDS WHO HAVE THE NEED.
YEAH, BUT WHICH OF THEM DID THE DEED?
WORK IT OUT!

*(***ALL** *freeze. Unfreeze* **DANNY** *with* **TJ** *and* **SQUEAK***.)*

DANNY. So, you played Frisbee by yourselves? There are no witnesses?

SQUEAK. Well, there were…

TJ. *(Nudging* **SQUEAK.***)* No witnesses. The park was empty.

DANNY. But it was a beautiful day. There must have been someone there.

TJ. Nope, nobody. And it was a rotten day, actually, 'cause I lost my Frisbee.

SQUEAK. I bet somebody stole it.

DANNY. Somebody at Monroe Park?

TJ. We told you – no one was there. Man, you are, like, stubborn as a fox.

DANNY. Better than being clever as a mule.

ENSEMBLE.
>HERE'S YOUR ASSIGNMENT, BABY:
>DIG UP ALL THE FACTS AND GET THE…TRUTH!
>IT TAKES REFINEMENT, BABY,
>IF YOU WANNA BE AN EXPERT SLEUTH.
>
>JUST BE CONFIDENT, COOL AND CHILL,
>AND RELY ON YOUR WIT AND SKILL…

GROUP 1.
>AND THEN YOU WILL
>WORK IT OUT!

GROUP 2.
>WORK IT OUT!

>*(***ALL*** freeze. Unfreeze* **PARKER** *with* **BECCA** *and* **OLIVE.***)*

PARKER. What are you making for your project?

OLIVE. We're still not sure. But we have plenty of art supplies.

BECCA. Yeah. The store gave me whatever I wanted – just so I'd leave and stop breaking stuff.

(They freeze. Unfreeze **ZAK** *with* **VICTORIA** *and* **WINSTON**.*)*

WINSTON. I was listening to my antique records.

VICTORIA. You and your crummy old records. I'd rather listen to Caliente 98!

ZAK. I love that radio station!

WINSTON. *(Unimpressed.)* Eh…the lobby is nice.

ZAK. You've been inside Caliente 98?

WINSTON. Of course. Daddy owns it.

ENSEMBLE.
TAKE A NOTE OF EV'RY SINGLE WORD THEY SAY.
JUST A TINY SLIP'LL GIVE THE CROOK AWAY…

TWO SOLOISTS.
HEY…

(All freeze. Unfreeze **PARKER** *and the* **ARTISTS**.*)*

PARKER. And what color paint are you using?

GUTHRIE. Blue. I chose the exact same shade as *Expression*.

ISABEL. I'm using lots of colors, but I borrowed that blue from Guthrie.

FRANCIS. Me, too. And I gave some to that annoying kid.

GUTHRIE. You know, the one nobody likes.

PARKER. *(Looking at* **TJ**.*)* Yeah, I know.

(They freeze. Unfreeze **JESS** *with* **SKATER(S)**, **ABBY** *and* **UNA**.*)*

JESS. So you were the only two in Monroe Park?

EMMETT. Pretty much. I skated for a while, and then I signed the Armstrongs' petition.*

---

*Throughout **EMMETT**'s line, change "I" to "we" if multiple **SKATERS**.

UNA. Written on 100% recycled paper!

ABBY. Then we saw TJ and Squeak ride by.

EMMETT. Wait – wasn't that on Monday?

ABBY. I thought it was Tuesday. Either way, it was the weirdest thing.

UNA. They rode by on their bikes, tossed a Frisbee into the park, and kept going.

JESS. Now, that's interesting...

ENSEMBLE.
> INVESTIGATION, BABY,
> TAKES A LITTLE LUCK AND LOTS OF...TIME!
> NO HESITATION, BABY,
> ZOOM IN ON YOUR TARGET, SOLVE THE CRIME.
>
> SO, JUST WHO COULD THE ROBBER BE?
> IS THERE SOMEONE WHO HOLDS THE KEY?
> IS IT SOMEBODY YOU CAN SEE?

GROUP 1.
> DON'T LOOK AT ME!
> TO SOLVE A MYSTERY...

GROUP 2.
> TO SOLVE A MYSTERY...

> *(Characters now unfreeze individually, as needed.)*

YVETTE. We're missing a canvas.

EMMETT. I'm missing a brush.

FRANCIS. *I'm* missing a brush.

ABBY. Missing purple.

GUTHRIE. Missing blue.

ISABEL. Missing...

KEISHA. Missing...

TJ. Missing the point. Who cares about this stuff, anyway?

ENSEMBLE.
WORK IT OUT!

(All exit, except **VICTORIA**, **WINSTON** *and* **GUMBALL GANG.***)*

[MUSIC NO. 09A – WORK IT OUT PLAYOFF]

Scene Nine: Victoria, Winston & The Gang

CANDY. Victoria, Winston, everyone in town is missing something except for the two of you.

WINSTON. So? Is it our fault we keep track of our belongings?

DANNY. Of course not. We just thought that was a little strange.

VICTORIA. You know what? I think you guys are only investigating us 'cause you're jealous.

DANNY. Jealous?

VICTORIA. Yes, of my beauty and fame!

WINSTON. And my money!

VICTORIA. And really, who could blame you? After all, we are fabulous!

[MUSIC NO. 10 – ALL FOR ME]

I'M HOT!
EV'RYONE KNOWS I'M GOING FAR!
I'VE GOT
ALL THAT IT TAKES TO BE A STAR!
A PAGEANT EV'RY WEEKEND,
COMMERCIALS ON TV.
IT'S ULTRA-CHIC AND
IT'S ALL FOR ME!
CHEER ME!
BABY, THAT'S WHAT THE PEOPLE DO.
REVERE ME,
SAYING I'M PERFECT THROUGH AND THROUGH!
THEY CALL FOR MY ATTENTION,
THEY WAIT IN LINE TO SEE.
AND DID I MENTION
IT'S ALL FOR ME?

JUST HEARING MY NAME BRINGS EUPHORIA.
OOH, VICTORIA!
I WAS BORN FOR FAME.
I SHOULD BE ENDORSING SOME CHARITY
'CAUSE POPULARITY
IS MY MIDDLE NAME!

Really! Victoria Popularity LaSalle.

MONEY,
POWER AND FAME KEEP ME ALIVE.
HONEY,
WATCH AS I RULE THIS BUSY HIVE!
SO BUZZ OFF, ALL YOU WORKERS.
YOU'RE LOOKING AT QUEEN BEE!

THE GLAMOUR AND THE GLITZ,
THE PAPARAZZI BLITZ,
I LOVE IT ALL, 'CAUSE IT'S ALL FOR ME!

WINSTON. Step aside, Victoria, and see how it's done.

NEWS FLASH –
DADDY OWNS HALF OF LITTLETOWN.
HIS CASH
MADE AN ESTATE OF GREAT RENOWN!

WE JET OFF TO AN ISLAND,
OR WEEKEND IN PAREE!
IT'S ALL IN STYLE AND
IT'S ALL FOR ME!

SO GIVE ME A LIFE OF PROSPERITY!
IN ALL SINCERITY,
POVERTY'S A BORE.

SINCE I'M FILTHY RICH AS A QUEEN OR KING,
I NEVER CLEAN A THING –
THAT'S WHAT THE MAID IS FOR!

It's so hard to find good help.
NO WAY
I WILL GIVE UP MY POSH ROUTINE.

WINSTON.
I SAY,
GIMME MY POOL AND LIMOUSINE!
SEE, MONEY IS MY PASSION...

VICTORIA.
HEY, WINSTON, I AGREE!

VICTORIA & WINSTON.
WE'LL NEVER CALL IT QUITS
TO DINING AT THE RITZ.
WE LOVE IT ALL...

WINSTON.
'CAUSE IT'S ALL FOR ME!

VICTORIA. *(Spoken in rhythm.)*
AND ME!

(Dance break: Four counts of eight.)

VICTORIA & WINSTON.
WE DON'T
CARE IF YOU THINK WE'VE GOT A LOT!
WE WON'T
EVER GET TIRED OF WHAT WE'VE GOT:

VICTORIA.
THE FANS WHO LONG TO SEE
MY NAME ON THAT MARQUEE!

WINSTON.
A CLASSY LIFE THAT'S FREE
FROM THE PETTY BOURGEOISIE,

VICTORIA & WINSTON.
AND SIMPLY KNOWING WE
ARE WHAT YOU WISH YOU COULD BE
HELPS US SEE
LIFE IS MEANT TO BE
ALL FOR ME!

VICTORIA.
FOR ME!

WINSTON.
FOR ME!

VICTORIA.
FOR ME!

VICTORIA & WINSTON.
FOR ME!!

DANNY. I've heard enough. Let's head back to the store.

ZAK. I'll be with you in a sec.

PARKER. Okay, see you later.

(**CANDY, DANNY, JESS** *and* **PARKER** *exit.*)

ZAK. You know, you guys are really good! Victoria, no wonder you win all those contests!

VICTORIA. Thank you, Zak.

ZAK. With a voice like that, you'll be on Caliente 98 in no time!

VICTORIA. You think? Maybe you could, too. See, Winston, *someone* here appreciates me.

WINSTON. What do you mean by that?

VICTORIA. *(To* **ZAK.***)* Winston refuses to finish his sketch of me. He doesn't appreciate a good subject.

ZAK. You're sketching her? May I see?

WINSTON. It's really not done yet, and I...

(**VICTORIA** *passes the sketch to* **ZAK.***)*

ZAK. *(Genuinely impressed.)* Whoa...Winston, this is beautiful. You have real talent.

WINSTON. You think so?

ZAK. Uh huh.

WINSTON. Thanks, Zak. I'm actually a little afraid to show my art to people.

ZAK. Well, you shouldn't be. You're a true artist.

VICTORIA. Of course he is! With a beautiful subject like me, even someone with no talent – like *you!* – could be an artist.

>   (**ZAK** *looks stunned.*)

Oh, don't feel bad, Zak...not everyone can be talented. I'm sure there's *something* about you that people like... (*Trying to make a joke.*) Though I can't imagine what that is.

>   (**VICTORIA** *looks at* **ZAK**, *expecting him to laugh. Instead,* **ZAK** *looks back in silence, hurt.*)

ZAK. Wow. You know, Victoria, for a second there, I thought we could be friends, but now I know / that you just can't.

VICTORIA. (*Flippant.*) Zak, what's the big deal? I was only / joking...

ZAK. Maybe someday you'll think of someone besides yourself, Victoria. Till then, you'll never have any *real* friends. (*To* **WINSTON**.) Good luck in the contest, Winston. I'm sure you'll do great. Bye.

>   (**ZAK** *exits as* **WINSTON** *and* **VICTORIA** *stare at each other in shock.* **TJ** *and* **SQUEAK**, *who had obviously been hiding, suddenly appear.*)

TJ. What was that?

>   (**TJ**, **SQUEAK**, **WINSTON** *and* **VICTORIA** *exit.*)

>   **[MUSIC NO. 10A – GUMBALL TRANSITION 2]**

Scene Ten: The Candy Store

(**CANDY, DANNY, JESS, PARKER** *and* **ZAK** *are brainstorming again.*)

CANDY. I'm stumped. Looks like everyone had access to something required for this crime.

(**BECCA** *and* **OLIVE** *enter.* **OLIVE** *is completely covered in dripping paint.*)

BECCA. Olive, I am SOOO sorry. Really. It was an accident. I am so embarrassed. Please, please, don't hate me. Olive? Olive, say something.

(*Everyone waits for* **OLIVE** *to speak. Finally…*)

OLIVE. That…was…AWESOME!

(*Everyone laughs.*)

PARKER. What happened?

OLIVE. I was lying down, drawing on a big sheet, while Becca was on a ladder, painting.

BECCA. Then a bee flew in. I totally freaked out and started swatting my paintbrush.

OLIVE. Next thing I knew, I was covered by Becca, the ladder…

BECCA. And a gallon of paint.

OLIVE. If you think I look bad, you should see the sheet. The only clean spot is the part I was covering.

BECCA. Olive – that's it!

OLIVE. What's it?

BECCA. I know what we should do for the contest! Come on, we've got a big mess to make.

OLIVE. A mess? Well, that is your specialty.

  (**BECCA** *and* **OLIVE** *exit past the* **REPORTERS** *and* **ZAK**, *who do a take, then continue into the Candy Store.*)

LYDIA. So, Candy, did you catch the crook yet?

CANDY. Nope, still no luck.

MORGAN. But it's already Thursday. Can you at least give us some details for tonight's segment?

PARKER. There's not much to tell. Everybody has a motive. Most people have an alibi.

CANDY. Except TJ and Squeak. Their "Frisbee in the park" story doesn't quite add up.

DANNY. And the fake painting? Just about anyone could have made it.

JESS. True. Lots of people had blue, white or purple paint. Several suspects had round objects that could be traced, and a canvas was missing from the museum.

CANDY. So, the thief could have taken that blank canvas, painted a fake, signed the back, and replaced the masterpiece when everyone else was busy preparing for the contest.

JESS. Of course, the thief made one mistake...using the wrong color for the signature.

LYDIA. Yes, the famous purple signature. Have you – or the police – had any luck finding the real one with the red signature?

DANNY. Nope, the masterpiece is still missing.

ZAK. I hope this doesn't discourage people from finishing their entries.

MORGAN. I doubt it. I can think of three artists in particular who are taking this contest very seriously...

(All nod as lights fade on the Candy Store.)

[MUSIC NO. 10B – MASTERPIECE TRANSITION]

Scene Eleven: Artists at Work

(The three **ART STUDENTS** *are working on their projects.)*

FRANCIS. Voilà! My project is finished.

ISABEL. I'm almost there.

GUTHRIE. Me, too. So, tell us about your project, Francis.

FRANCIS. Oh, I couldn't. I'm far too modest.

ISABEL. Please…

[MUSIC NO. 11 – IT'S A MASTERPIECE]

FRANCIS. If you insist.
JUST LOOK AT THIS PAINTING, SO DELICATE AND LIGHT.
THE DAPPLING OF COLOR IN BLUE, PINK, AND WHITE.

IT'S GENTLE AND AIRY AND COOL AS THE SEA.
MY ELEGANT USE OF THE BRUSH IS THE KEY!

(Spoken in rhythm.)
WILL IT TAKE FIRST PRIZE TOMORROW? *MAIS OUI!*

(Sung.)

IT'S A MASTERPIECE!
SUCH A FINE WORK OF ART.
IT'S A MASTERPIECE,
FULL OF ROMANCE AND HEART.
WHEN THEY SEE IT,
THEY'LL AGREE IT IS WORTH
ITS OWN WEIGHT IN GOLD.

IT'S SO BEAUTIFUL,
LIKE THE GREATS LONG AGO.
TRULY BEAUTIFUL,
AN ENCHANTING TABLEAU!

AND SO CLEVER!
WHO COULD EVER HAVE GUESSED
I WOULD PAINT LIKE THE MASTERS OF OLD?
IT'S A MASTERPIECE!
SUCH A BEAUTIFUL THING TO BEHOLD!

ISABEL. It is lovely. So different from mine.

GUTHRIE. Tell us about it.

ISABEL. Oh, I couldn't sing my own praises. But, if I must…
LOOK AT THE FRUIT OF MY LABOR!
IT'S A PERFECT DEPICTION OF SORROW AND JOY ON EACH
    FACE.
IT'S YOUR MOTHER, YOUR FATHER,
YOUR SISTER, YOUR BROTHER, YOUR NEIGHBOR!
WHEN I CELEBRATE PEOPLE, I HONOR THE WHOLE
    HUMAN RACE!
IT'S A MASTERPIECE!
IT'S SO HONEST AND TRUE.
IT'S A MASTERPIECE,
WITH A CLEAR POINT OF VIEW,
AND SO NOBLE!
IT HAS GLOBAL APPEAL WITH A STORY THAT BEGS TO BE
    TOLD.
IT'S A MASTERPIECE!
SUCH A BEAUTIFUL THING TO BEHOLD!

GUTHRIE. Wonderful work, Isabel.

ISABEL. Thanks, Guthrie. And what have you created?

GUTHRIE. Oh, just a little something…
CHROME AND GLASS.
NEON GAS.
MODERN LIFE, PAIN AND STRIFE, DARK AND SLEEK.
TECHNO SCENE.
SHARP AND CLEAN.
CLANGING GONG, STURM UND DRANG, HARD AND CHIC!

GUTHRIE.
> IT'S A STATEMENT,
> SAYING LIFE IS HOLLOW AND COLD.
> IT'S A MASTERPIECE!
> SUCH A BEAUTIFUL THING TO BEHOLD!

FRANCIS. Superb, Guthrie.

GUTHRIE. Thanks. But it's out of my hands.

FRANCIS. Yup. It's up to the judges now.

ISABEL. We'll all just have to stay humble.

> (**FRANCIS** and **GUTHRIE** nod, then all three sing.)

FRANCIS.

IT'S A	**ISABEL.**	**GUTHRIE.**
MASTERPIECE!	LOOK...	CHROME AND GLASS.
SUCH A FINE WORK OF ART! IT'S A	AT THE FRUIT OF MY	NEON GAS. MODERN LIFE. PAIN AND STRIFE.
MASTERPIECE! FULL OF ROMANCE AND HEART,	LABOR!	DARK AND SLEEK.
WHEN THEY SEE IT	IT'S A PERFECT	TECHNO SCENE.
THEY'LL AGREE	DEPICTION OF	SHARP AND CLEAN.
IT IS WORTH	SORROW AND	CLANGING GONG.
ITS OWN	JOY TO	STURM UND DRANG.
WEIGHT IN GOLD.	UNFOLD.	HARD AND COLD.

IT'S SO
   BEAUTIFUL,
LIKE THE
   GREATS
LONG AGO!
TRULY

BEAUTIFUL AN
ENCHANTING
   TABLEAU!
AND SO
   CLEVER!
WHO COULD

EVER HAVE

GUESSED I
   WOULD
PAINT
LIKE THE
MASTERS OF
OLD?

LOOK!

IT'S YOUR
MOTHER OR

NEIGHBOR!

IT'S SO NOBLE
AND
IT HAS A

GLOBAL APPEAL

WITH A

STORY THAT

BEGS TO BE
TOLD.

CHROME AND
   GLASS.
NEON GAS.

MODERN LIFE.
PAIN AND
   STRIFE.
DARK AND
   SLEEK.

TECHNO SCENE.

SHARP AND
   CLEAN.
CLANGING
   GONG.

STURM UND
   DRANG.
LIFE THAT IS

HOLLOW AND
   COLD!

FRANCIS, ISABEL & GUTHRIE.
IT'S A MASTERPIECE!
SUCH A BEAUTIFUL THING TO BEHOLD!
IT'S A MASTERPIECE!
SUCH A BEAUTIFUL THING TO BEHOLD!

[MUSIC NO. 11A – MASTERPIECE PLAYOFF]

Scene Twelve: The Candy Store

(**CANDY** *is pacing as* **PARKER**, **JESS** *and* **ZAK** *look through their notes.*)

CANDY. So, anything to report?

JESS. The circle in the painting is twelve inches wide. Nothing we've found is that size.

CANDY. Right, so we can cross off Victoria's tiara...

ZAK. Six inches.

CANDY. Emmett's CD...

JESS. Five inches.

PARKER. And TJ's brain...two inches.

CANDY. Easy, now.

(**DANNY** *comes running in.*)

DANNY. Hey, how about TJ's Frisbee?

ZAK. You just ran all the way from Monroe Park?

DANNY. I didn't win the state track finals for nothing, you know.

JESS. Well, your running is amazing, Danny, but unfortunately this Frisbee is nine inches. Cross it off the list.

PARKER. Actually, we can cross off everything, because a compass makes a circle any size, and they're easy to get. I keep one here. (*Looking around.*) Wait, where is it?

CANDY. I still think it's one of Winston's records.

JESS. Could be, but lots of people have records.

(*Suddenly,* **TJ** *and* **SQUEAK** *appear, followed by the* **REPORTERS**.)

TJ. But not records with blue paint around the edges!

DANNY. TJ!

SQUEAK. *(Correcting him.)* And Squeak!

DANNY. And Squeak. What are you doing here?

TJ. We're here to say the Dumbball Gang actually stole that painting, and we can prove it!

SQUEAK. *(To the* **REPORTERS**.*)* Make sure you get this.

TJ. So, Granny, why don't you show us what's hiding over there?

> (**DANNY** *discovers a twelve-inch LP with blue paint around the edges.)*

DANNY. It's an old Stan Kenton record.

TJ. See? They obviously traced that record to make the phony painting.

LYDIA. Candy, is this true? Why'd you do it – for the publicity?

CANDY. Of course it isn't true.

MORGAN. Sorry guys, but you better produce some evidence, or we'll have to show the police.

JESS. What kind of evidence?

> (**VICTORIA** *and* **WINSTON** *storm in.)*

VICTORIA. How about a character witness?

WINSTON. Or two!

SQUEAK. What are you doing here?

TJ. Go away, you guys are messing this up!

WINSTON. I know that record...it was mine. Look at the "B" side – my name is on it.

DANNY. There it is: Winston Winston the Third.

TJ. So? That just proves they stole it from him!

WINSTON. *(To* **TJ.***)* How could they steal it from me when I gave it to you?

TJ. Are you nuts? Why are you saying that out loud?

VICTORIA. We're sorry, guys. Winston gave TJ that record, and I gave him some blue paint I got from Francis.

PARKER. So *you're* the kid nobody likes. Hah. I thought they meant TJ.

> *(***VICTORIA*** pauses to process this for a second.)*

VICTORIA. Anyway, TJ wanted to frame the Gumball Gang, and we helped him. We're so sorry.

DANNY. *(To* **TJ.***)* So that's what you were doing when you claimed to be in Monroe Park...setting us up!

CANDY. You biked so quickly, you had plenty of time to stop by here and hide that record.

PARKER. But you slowed down just enough to throw a Frisbee into the park...

JESS. So we'd find it and think you spent the day there.

SQUEAK. Smart, huh? That was my idea.

TJ. *(To* **VICTORIA** *and* **WINSTON.***)* Why did you have to ruin it? Everything was going so good.

CANDY. Of course, you did that on Tuesday, AFTER the painting was stolen, right? Or was it actually on Monday, BEFORE the crime was committed?

TJ. Hey, I may be a liar and a cheat, but I'm not a thief!

LYDIA. Care to say that to the press? Come on, TJ...

SQUEAK. And Squeak!

LYDIA. And Squeak. We've got an exclusive interview to do.

(*TJ,* **SQUEAK** *and the* **REPORTERS** *exit.*)

DANNY. So, we found the thief?

CANDY. Maybe. But I'm not sure it's TJ. I have to do some research and get back to you.

(*She consults her phone.*)

VICTORIA. Zak, I thought about what you said, and you're right. I mean, I'm fabulous and all, but I guess I could be fabulous *and* a little nicer.

WINSTON. Me too.

[MUSIC NO. 12 – LIFE IS SWEET]

And you know what's weird? I feel a lot better for some reason.

ZAK. I know why.
WHEN YOU'RE SPLITTING A SANDWICH WITH A BUDDY,
OH, LIFE IS SWEET.
WHEN YOU'RE LENDING A HAND TO HELP THEM STUDY,
OH, LIFE IS SWEET!

SHARE A LITTLE OF WHAT IS YOURS
WITH A FRIEND YOU'D LIKE TO MEET.
START BY OPENING LOTS OF DOORS
OR BY HELPING SOMEONE CROSS THE STREET!

CANDY.
WHEN YOU WELCOME THE NEW KID TO YOUR TABLE,

VICTORIA, WINSTON & GUMBALL GANG (ALL).
OH, LIFE IS SWEET.

DANNY.
WHEN YOU HONESTLY DO THE BEST YOU'RE ABLE,

ALL.
OH, LIFE IS SWEET!

ZAK.

GIVE A LITTLE OF WHAT'S IN YOU,
AND A CIRCLE IS COMPLETE.

ALL (EXCEPT ZAK).

SWEET...

ZAK.

ALL THE NEGATIVE THINGS YOU KNEW
WILL BE SPARKLING LIKE GLITTER,
'CAUSE THE THINGS THAT ONCE WERE BITTER
NOW ARE SWEET...

PARKER.

WHEN YOU VOLUNTEER TO MAKE THINGS BETTER,

ALL.

OH, LIFE IS SWEET.

JESS.

WHEN YOU WRITE A SINCERE AND THOUGHTFUL LETTER,

ALL.

OH, LIFE IS SWEET...

ZAK.

BEING FRIENDLY AND FAIR AND NICE
ISN'T ALL THAT HARD TO DO.

ALL.

SWEET...

ZAK.

MAKE THE TINIEST SACRIFICE
AND THE THINGS YOU GIVE COME BACK TO YOU!

VICTORIA.

WHEN YOU TRY TO BE KIND, POLITE AND PLEASANT,

ALL.

OH, LIFE IS SWEET.

WINSTON.

WHEN YOU'RE SHOPPING TO FIND THE PERFECT
    PRESENT,

ALL.

OH, LIFE IS SWEET.

VICTORIA, WINSTON & ZAK.

GIVE A LITTLE OF WHAT'S IN YOU
AND A CIRCLE IS COMPLETE.

GUMBALL GANG (EXCEPT ZAK).

SWEET...

VICTORIA, WINSTON & ZAK.

ALL THE NEGATIVE THINGS YOU KNEW

VICTORIA.

WILL BE BLOOMING LIKE A FLOWER,

WINSTON.

'CAUSE THE THINGS THAT ONCE WERE SOUR

ALL.

NOW ARE SWEET...
OH, LIFE IS SWEET.

CANDY. Well, I'm glad everyone made up, because I know
who did it.

DANNY. You do?

CANDY. Yeah, but they're about to announce the contest
winner. Let's go!

[MUSIC NO. 12A – GUMBALL TRANSITION 3]

Scene Thirteen: Museum Steps (Conclusion)

(The **REPORTERS** *address the audience as everyone, except the* **GUMBALL GANG**, *gathers behind them.)*

MORGAN. It's Friday afternoon. Welcome to the Channel Three debut of *Littletown Live!*

LYDIA. We're reaching a statewide audience with this broadcast!

MORGAN. It's time for the big announcement.

YVETTE. Ladies and Gentlemen...

[MUSIC NO. 12B – COSMOPOLITAN FINE ART SHOW (REPRISE)]

We are pleased to announce the winners of...

JUDGES.
THE COSMOPOLITAN FINE ART SHOW
AND AMATEUR COMPETITION!

YVETTE. And the winners are...

*(***GUMBALL GANG*** enters.)*

CANDY. Hold it!! Wait!

KEISHA. What? What's going on?

*(***CANDY*** takes the stage and addresses the crowd.)*

CANDY. Ladies and Gentlemen, my name is Candy Krunch, and I'm here to tell you we've solved the Case of the Missing Masterpiece!

(The **CROWD** *gasps.)*

LYDIA. This is a first! The Gumball Gang, solving a crime right here on *Littletown Live!*

CANDY. In fact, the thief is right here among us.

ZAK. There were several suspects, including: Victoria LaSalle…

[MUSIC NO. 12C – ACCUSATIONS]

(An organ sounds an ominous chord, and **VICTORIA** *strikes a pose as the others look at her. The same happens with each subsequent accusation.)*

…who resented the painting for stealing her spotlight;

PARKER. Winston Winston the Third *(Music: chord.)*, who felt that only someone of his class deserved such a treasure;

JESS. Abby and Una Armstrong, *(Chord.)* who protested the unveiling of the painting;

CANDY. Emmett Hanley, *(Chord.)* who was always seeking a new thrill;*

DANNY. TJ Doyle

SQUEAK. And Squeak!

DANNY. …and Squeak, *(Chord.)* who love to stir up any kind of trouble;

ZAK. Becca Krunch, *(Chord.)* who needed to prove she could do something right;

CANDY. And three visiting youth artists: Francis, *(Chord.)* Isabel, *(Chord.)* and Guthrie, *(Chord.)* who each knew the painting's true worth.

PARKER. Of course, we were suspects as well, and so were the contest judges. *(Chord.)*

---

* Substitute with "The skaters, who were always seeking a new thrill," if cast includes multiple skaters.

JESS. All of these people had access to the objects necessary to create a fake painting.

CANDY. But in the end, it was something someone said that gave away the crime. I had to do some research to confirm my theory, and now I'm certain.

DANNY. When the fake painting was revealed, the judges said the signature was wrong – it was purple.

ZAK. We later learned that the real signature was red.

CANDY. But the judges swore they never told anyone but us, and I couldn't find that information online, in the museum catalog, or in the library.

PARKER. Only the thief could know that. So the thief is actually someone we *haven't* mentioned.

BECCA. Oh, my gosh – Olive...you stole the masterpiece?

OLIVE. What? No!

CANDY. Olive didn't steal it...the *reporters* did!

(*The* **CROWD** *gasps.*)

JESS. They interviewed every single person here...

PARKER. And when they did, they took a flash picture, which distracted people just long enough for the reporters to steal what they needed:

DANNY. The museum's canvas, Parker's compass...

ZAK. Blue, white and purple paint from the artists, Becca and Abby...

JESS. A thin brush from Francis, and a wide brush from Emmett!

CANDY. Apparently, they were so desperate for a good story that they had to create one themselves. So... Lydia, Morgan, what do you have to say now?

MORGAN. Fine. You're right, we did it.

LYDIA. We couldn't pass up the chance to make it to national news!

PARKER. Well, you're definitely gonna make the national news *now*.

MORGAN. We're sorry – it wasn't about the money, and we honestly didn't want to hurt anyone.

LYDIA. And we were planning to give it back.

EMMETT. I don't get it... you obviously hid the stolen objects in that big bag, but where's the painting?

LYDIA. Right here...

> (**LYDIA** *removes the "Littletown Live!" card to reveal the painting. The* **JUDGES** *immediately reclaim it.)*

YVETTE. We'll take that, thank you!

MORGAN. Don't worry. We're going to the police to turn ourselves in.

LYDIA. But first, please...let us file one last report.

MORGAN. Our final segment on the Missing Masterpiece. Ready, Lydia?

LYDIA. Ready. So, Candy Krunch, you solved the case –

[MUSIC NO. 13 – CASE CLOSED]

of the Missing Masterpiece. You did it.

CANDY. I didn't do it...we did.

> WE DID IT, TRUE, BUT KEEP IN MIND
> WE DID IT WITH OUR SKILLS COMBINED!

PARKER & ZAK.
> ADMIT IT – WE CAN ONLY FIND
> A CROOK, OR CRACK A SCHEME,

GUMBALL GANG.
WHEN WE'RE WORKING AS A TEAM!
AND WE DID IT!
WE TOUGHED IT OUT AND TRIED OUR VERY BEST!
WE DID IT!
WITHOUT A DOUBT, WE PASSED THE FINAL TEST.
AND WHEN WE ALL WORKED TOGETHER,
THOSE TWO ROBBERS WERE EXPOSED.
AND THEY ADMIT IT...
CASE CLOSED.

EMMETT.   But wait! We still don't know who won the contest.

CANDY.   That's right. Madame Judges?

KEISHA.   Thank you, Candy. The Cosmopolitan is pleased to announce our winners.

RHONDA.   In third place: Guthrie Bildhauer, for her sculpture entitled *The Thrill of Boredom*.

> *(Guthrie's sculpture is revealed. The others, especially* **ISABEL** *and* **FRANCIS**, *congratulate her.)*

GUTHRIE.   Thank you! I owe it all to my fellow artists.

YVETTE.   In second place: Winston Winston the Third, for his *Portrait of Two Friends*.

> *(* **JUDGES** *reveal a lovely sketch of* **ZAK** *and* **VICTORIA** *looking very friendly together. Everyone cheers, especially* **ZAK** *and* **VICTORIA**.*)*

WINSTON.   Wow, thanks! I share this honor with my friends, Zak and Victoria.

RHONDA.   And the Grand Prize goes to...

KEISHA.   Becca and Olive Krunch, for their expressive work entitled *Make a Splash!*

(The **JUDGES** *reveal a colorful collage of life-sized silhouettes in active poses. The figures are in negative space surrounded by splattered paint. The* **JUDGES** *present* **BECCA** *and* **OLIVE** *with an oversized check for "One Year's Supply of Candy.")*

KEISHA. Tell us, winners, how did you choose this project?

BECCA. Gosh, I don't know.

OLIVE. It just sort of...hit me.

BECCA.
WE WON IT! I CAN'T BELIEVE IT'S TRUE!

OLIVE.
WE WON IT, BECCA, ME AND YOU!

VICTORIA, WINSTON & ART STUDENTS.
WE'VE DONE IT! AND WE MADE IT THROUGH
BY PROVING YOU'LL GO FAR
WHEN YOU STAY TRUE TO WHO YOU ARE!

BECCA, OLIVE, VICTORIA, WINSTON & ART STUDENTS.
AND WE DID IT!
WE HELPED A FRIEND AND TRIED OUR VERY BEST.
WE DID IT!
AND IN THE END, WE PASSED THE FINAL TEST!
BEING WHO YOU ARE IS EASY,
NOT AS HARD AS WE SUPPOSED.
THAT'S HOW WE DID IT...
CASE CLOSED.

TJ & SQUEAK.
WE HAD A CHANCE TO MAKE THOSE GUMBALL KIDS
    LOOK BAD.

REPORTERS.
WE HAD TO GO AND BLOW THE BEST REPORT WE HAD.

TJ, SQUEAK & REPORTERS.
WHY COULDN'T WE DO IT?

(Spoken in rhythm.)
WE BLEW IT!

ABBY. *(To* **UNA.***)* Well, I guess it's another lost cause for us, too.

YVETTE. Ladies and Gentlemen, I've just been informed that, thanks to an anonymous donation, the Museum will soon open...The Armstrong Wildlife Refuge!

KEISHA. With an information and support center for endangered animals...

RHONDA. Including the Blue-Tailed Skink!

ZAK. *(To* **WINSTON.***)* Anonymous donation?

(WINSTON *slyly shrugs.)*

VICTORIA. Why, Winston, you old softie.

PROTESTORS.
WHO KNEW IT? SOMEONE HEARD US SING!
WE GOT TO IT, AND I BET BY SPRING
THEY'LL DO IT – THEY WILL BUILD THAT WING.
AND SOMEDAY, WORLD, JUST THINK...
WE MIGHT SAVE THE BLUE-TAILED SKINK!

SKATER(S).
SOMEONE'S DOING JUST EXACTLY WHAT YOU PROPOSED!

PROTESTORS & SKATER(S).
CASE CLOSED.

JUDGES.
THIS COMPETITION HAS SCORED A PERFECT TEN!
AND SO, WE VOW, ONE YEAR FROM NOW,
WE'RE DOING IT ALL AGAIN!

PROTESTORS & SKATER(S).
WE DID OUR PART...

ARTISTS, BECCA & OLIVE.
WE MADE GREAT ART...

REPORTERS, TJ & SQUEAK.
WE MADE AMENDS...

VICTORIA, WINSTON & ZAK.
WE MADE NEW FRIENDS...

JUDGES.
RAN THE CONTEST ON A DIME!

GUMBALL GANG.
GOT THE MASTERPIECE IN TIME!

ALL.
AND IT'S ALL BECAUSE THE GUMBALL GANG
WAS HERE TO SOLVE THE CRIME!

ALL (EXCEPT REPORTERS).
AND WE ALL DID IT!
WE TOUGHED IT OUT AND TRIED OUR VERY BEST!
WE DID IT!
WITHOUT A DOUBT, WE PASSED THE FINAL TEST!
AND WHEN WE ALL WORK TOGETHER,
WE ARE MORE THAN WE SUPPOSED.
THAT'S HOW WE DID IT.
ADMIT IT!

REPORTERS.
WE DID IT...

MORGAN. Well, there you have it. The Gumball Gang has solved another case.

LYDIA. And we're going to Juvenile Detention! Till we're paroled, this is Lydia Lee...

MORGAN. And Morgan McCorgan.

CANDY. And this is...

GUMBALL GANG. The Gumball Gang!

ALL.
CASE CLOSED!
CASE CLOSED!
CASE CLOSED!

(Shouted.)

WE DID IT!

[MUSIC NO. 14 – BOWS]

ALL.
CASE CLOSED!
CASE CLOSED!
CASE CLOSED!

(Shouted.)

WE DID IT!

[MUSIC NO. 15 – EXIT MUSIC]

The End